READING RAINBOW® READERS

D1541320

ADVENTURE STORIES

THAT WILL THRILL YOU

SeaStar Books

NEW YORK

Special thanks to Amy Cohn, Leigh Ann Jones, Valerie Lewis, and Walter Mayes for the consultation services and invaluable support they provided for the creation of this book.

Reading Rainbow® is a production of GPN/Nebraska ETV and WNED-TV Buffalo and is produced by Lancit Media Entertainment, Ltd., a JuniorNet Company. *Reading Rainbow®* is a registered trademark of GPN/WNED-TV.

The following are gratefully acknowledged for granting permission to reprint the material in this book: "Dragons and Giants" from *Frog and Toad Together.* Copyright © 1971 by Arnold Lobel. Used by permission of HarperCollins Publishers. • "The Explorer" from *Lionel in the Winter* by Stephen Krensky, illustrated by Susanna Natti. Text copyright © 1994 by Stephen Krensky. Illustrations copyright © 1994 by Susanna Natti. Used by permission of Dial Books for Young Readers, a division of Penguin Putnam Inc. • "Eye of the Storm" from *Beezy* by Megan McDonald, illustrated by Nancy Poydar. Text copyright © 1997 by Megan McDonald. Illustrations copyright © 1997 by Nancy Poydar. Used by permission of Orchard Books. • "The Wild Animal" from *The Joy Boys* by Betsy Byars, illustrated by Frank Remkiewicz. Text copyright © 1996 by Betsy Byars. Illustrations copyright © 1996 by Frank Remkiewicz. Used by permission of Random House Children's Books, a division of Random House, Inc. • "The Sailboat" from *Poppleton Everyday* by Cynthia Rylant, illustrated by Mark Teague. Text copyright © 1998 by Cynthia Rylant. Illustrations copyright © 1998 by Mark Teague. Used by permission of Scholastic, Inc.

SeaStar Books • A division of North-South Books Inc.

ISBN 1-58717-101-5 (reinforced trade binding) 10 9 8 7 6 5 4 3 2 1
ISBN 1-58717-102-3 (paperback edition) 10 9 8 7 6 5 4 3 2 1

CONTENTS

Dragons and Giants
by Arnold Lobel

Frog and Toad
were reading a book together.
"The people in this book
are brave," said Toad.
"They fight dragons and giants,
and they are never afraid."
"I wonder if we are brave,"
said Frog.
Frog and Toad looked into a mirror.

"We look brave," said Frog.

"Yes, but are we?"

asked Toad.

Frog and Toad went outside.
"We can try to climb this mountain,"
said Frog. "That should tell us
if we are brave."
Frog went leaping over rocks,
and Toad came puffing up
behind him.

They came to a dark cave.
A big snake came out of the cave.
"Hello lunch," said the snake
when he saw Frog and Toad.
He opened his wide mouth.
Frog and Toad jumped away.
Toad was shaking.
"I am not afraid!" he cried.

They climbed higher,
and they heard a loud noise.
Many large stones
were rolling down the mountain.
"It's an avalanche!" cried Toad.

Frog and Toad jumped away.

Frog was trembling.

"I am not afraid!" he shouted.

They came to the top
of the mountain.
The shadow of a hawk
fell over them.
Frog and Toad
jumped under a rock.
The hawk flew away.

"We are not afraid!"
screamed Frog and Toad
at the same time.
Then they ran down the mountain
very fast.
They ran past the place
where they saw the avalanche.
They ran past the place
where they saw the snake.
They ran all the way
to Toad's house.

"Frog, I am glad to have
a brave friend like you," said Toad.
He jumped into the bed
and pulled the covers
over his head.
"And I am happy to know
a brave person like you, Toad,"
said Frog.
He jumped into the closet
and shut the door.
Toad stayed in the bed
and Frog stayed in the closet.

They stayed there
for a long time,
just feeling very brave together.

The Explorer

by Stephen Krensky

pictures by Susanna Natti

Lord Lionel Snowshoe,
the Arctic explorer,
was crossing the frozen snow.
Nine strong huskies were pulling
his dogsled.
A storm had been raging for days.
Most explorers would have gotten
hopelessly lost.
But not Lord Lionel.

He kept his bearings.
"There's the North Pole," he said.
"I'd know it anywhere."
Suddenly he heard the sound
of rushing snow.

"Avalanche!" he cried.
Lord Lionel ducked down
and covered his head.
He hoped the avalanche
wouldn't bury him too deeply.

Luckily he always carried a shovel
in his pack.
It was important to be prepared
for the unexpected.
The Arctic was filled with dangers.
Lord Lionel stood up.

The avalanche had been a small one.
He brushed the snow off his shoulders
and looked around.
"Uh-oh," he said. "Grizzly bears!"
If they saw him, he was doomed.

Lord Lionel backed away slowly.

Suddenly he stopped.

A great crack had opened
in the snow.

"From a recent earthquake," he said.

He could not go around it.

Lord Lionel looked down.

He could not see the bottom.

"I'll have to jump across," he said.

There was no time to waste.

The crack could widen at any moment.

Lord Lionel released his huskies
so that they could jump across
by themselves.
Then he backed up
and took a great leap.
He landed safely on the other side.

"Lionel, time to eat,"
said the quartermaster
from his base camp.
The explorer sighed.
It was good to hear a friendly voice
after weeks of traveling in the wilderness.
"Coming," he said,
and went inside for lunch.

Eye of the Storm

by Megan McDonald
PICTURES BY Nancy Poydar

Knock knock.

"Someone is at the door,"
said Beezy.

"Just the wind," Gran said.

"Merlin!" said Beezy.

"We thought you were the wind."

Merlin was wet.

"I ran all the way
from my house," Merlin said.

"I ran six blocks to tell you
there might be a hurricane.
Right here in Soda Springs!"

"Your best friend is
out in the rain, Beezy," Gran said.
"Let him in."
Merlin dripped a puddle on the floor.
He dripped a puddle on the chair.
"Get Merlin a towel, Beezy."
Knock knock knock.

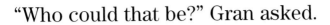
"Who could that be?" Gran asked.

"Just the rain," said Beezy.

"Gumm!" Gran said.

"We thought you
were the rain."

"I closed up shop," said Mr. Gumm.
"I ran three blocks to tell you
there might be a hurricane.
Right here in Soda Springs!"

"Gran," said Beezy.
"Your best friend is
out in the rain."

"I have candles," Mr. Gumm said.
"In case the lights go out."

"Scary," said Merlin.

"Spooky," said Beezy.

The lights blinked.
Off. On. Off. On.

The house went dark.

Gran lit the candles.

The candles made spooky shadows.

"Now what?" Beezy asked.

"We wait out the storm," Gran said.

"You mean hurricane," said Merlin.

"We can tell stories,"
Mr. Gumm said.

"Ghost stories!" said Beezy.

"Hurricane stories!" Merlin cried.

Mr. Gumm began:

"When I was just a boy

and your gran was just a girl—"

"You knew Gran back then?"

Beezy asked.

"I knew your gran
back in the days
when stones were soft."
"Wow," said Merlin.
"Yes, sir. Hurricane Jane. 1942.
She blew in up the coast
from the Florida Keys."

"Remember the red sky?"
Gran asked.
"Sunset as red as a beet,"
Mr. Gumm said.
"Winds faster than a car can drive."
"Wow," said Beezy.

"She could snap trees in half.
Lifted the roof right off the house!
We hid in the dark
and ate peanut butter crackers,"
said Mr. Gumm.
"Sang songs till it got quiet,"
Gran said.

"Eye of the storm," said Mr. Gumm.
"Until a wall of water
rolled down the street."
"Dropped a washing machine
right in the front yard," Gran said.
"Wow," said Merlin.

Beezy and Merlin
and Gran and Mr. Gumm
ate peanut butter crackers,
sang songs, and told stories
till the lights came on.
"The storm is over," Gran said.

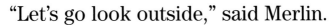

"Let's go look outside," said Merlin.
"I don't see any washing machines,"
said Beezy.
"Oh, well," Merlin said.
"Maybe we will have
another hurricane tomorrow."

THE WILD ANIMAL

BY Betsy Byars

PICTURES BY Frank Remkiewicz

"No Bono, you can't come with us,"
J.J. said.
"You have to go home."
Bono stopped.
His tail drooped.
"Yes," said Harry.
"A wild animal has been
after our sheep.
We have to catch him.

You will be in the way."

Bono sat down.

He watched J.J. and Harry walk off.

At the trees, the boys turned.

"Now don't follow us.

We mean it."

J.J. and Harry went

deep into the woods.

They stopped at the cliff.

"We can watch for the wild animal

here," Harry said.

"Let's put up the tent."

"And the campfire can go here," said J.J.
The boys worked hard,
but it got dark before supper was ready.
"We better eat in the tent," J.J. said.
Harry said, "Why?"

"Because of the wild animal."

Harry said, "What wild animal?"

"The wild animal
that's after the sheep."

Harry said, "Let's go in the tent."

They ate their food in the tent.

Then they lay down.

After a while Harry said,

"I can't sleep, can you, J.J.?"

J.J. said, "No."

Harry said,

"I keep thinking about the wild animal."

"I do too," said J.J.

Harry sat up.

"What was that?" he said.

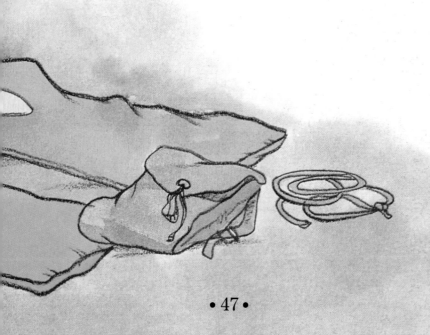

"What?"

"I heard something," Harry said.

"What?"

"It sounded like a wild animal."

They listened.

They heard footsteps.

They heard breathing.

The flap of the tent opened.

A long nose poked through the flap.

"Wild animal! Wild animal!"

Harry cried.

He pulled his sleeping bag over his head.

J.J. pulled his sleeping bag over his head.

They waited.

Then the long nose poked J.J.

J.J. peeked out.

"It's Bono! Bono!" he said.

"Harry, look, it's Bono.

He chased the wild animal away."

Bono lay down between the Joy boys.
"Now I can sleep, can't you?"
said Harry.
"Yes, now I can sleep," said J.J.
The Joy boys fell asleep
as Bono's tail wagged on the floor
of the tent.

THE SAILBOAT
BY Cynthia Rylant
PICTURES BY Mark Teague

Poppleton's friend Fillmore got
a new sailboat.

"Will you come sailing?"
asked Fillmore.

"Sure!" said Poppleton.

So he went in Fillmore's boat.

Poppleton had never been sailing.
He didn't know what to do.
"Do you know what to do, Fillmore?"
asked Poppleton.

"Sure," said Fillmore.
"Just sit back and relax."
Poppleton sat back.

Suddenly the boat leaned
to the far, far left.
"I am not relaxed, Fillmore!"
cried Poppleton.
The boat leaned to the far, far right.
"NOT RELAXED!" Poppleton cried.
"Relax!" said Fillmore.

Then the boat caught a strong wind.
It bounced up and down, up and down
on the waves.
"I AM NOT RELAXED!" cried Poppleton.

A big storm came.

"NOT RELAXED!" Poppleton cried.

Then the sailboat flipped over.

"DEFINITELY NOT RELAXED!"
cried Poppleton,
swimming beside Fillmore.
"Relax!" said Fillmore.

Poppleton and Fillmore climbed
back in the boat.

They sailed back to shore.

"Wasn't that fun?" asked Fillmore.

"Well, not all of it," said Poppleton.

"The leaning was fun, and the bouncing was fun, and the flipping over was fun," said Fillmore.

"Yes, but the shark wasn't," said Poppleton.
"SHARK!!!???" shouted Fillmore,
and he went screaming down the road.
"Gee, Fillmore," called Poppleton.
"RELAX!"

Then Poppleton went home, smiling, and did just that.